CW01090933

The Winter War

Written By: Cristian Lascau
Illustrated By: Emma Rusnac

The Winter War

Written By: Cristian Lascau
Illustrated By: Emma Rusnac

This book is dedicated to my two children, Oliver and Hope. Dont ever stop creating and using your imagination. Your imagination and your ability to dream are a gift that should never stop.

To my wife Renee: Thank you for always believing in me and for pushing me to create.

Table Of Contents

The Winter War

Chapter 1

In a small town in the Northwest, on a tiny street, lived a young boy named Tommy. He loved the winter season, especially when it snowed. It wasn't because he liked to go sledding or ice-skating, Tommy loved the snow because he loved to play pranks on his neighbor Mr.B. Now Mr.B was a quiet old man that lived alone and loved to keep his yard very clean. Mr.B didn't like the winter because of Tommy, especially when it snowed.

The first prank that started it all, was when Tommy was 7 years old. Tommy was playing in the front yard with his Dad and his best friend Teddy when he saw Mr.B come out to shovel his sidewalk. Tommy ran and hid behind his snowman and made a snowball. When Mr.B was in the perfect place on his sidewalk, Tommy threw the snowball up in the air as high as he could throw. The snowball came back down and landed straight on Mr.B's head, breaking in a million pieces of snow. Mr.B looked around and saw that Tommy was laughing on the floor with Teddy. Mr.B yelled at Tommy's dad, which in turn got Tommy in trouble. As Dad was apologizing to Mr.B, Tommy knew that this was the beginning of the Winter War.

Chapter 2

The next year, right after the first snowfall, Tommy ran outside and began to build a snowman. Teddy was sitting on the sled watching the snowman get built. The snow was falling hard and fast, which made it a perfect day for pranking Mr.B. When the snowman was completed, Tommy took Teddy and they both ducked behind the snowman and waited for Mr.B to come out of his house and start shoveling the sidewalk. The front door opened as Mr.B exited his house wearing a big brown coat and a leather hat with fur on the inside. Mr.B was carrying a shovel in his hands. As soon as he closed the door, Mr.B took a good look around his yard and Tommy's yard to see if anyone was outside. All Mr.B could see was a snowman that was freshly built in front of Tommy's house. Mr.B did not see Tommy and Teddy hiding behind the snowman and began to shovel the snow off of the sidewalk in front of his porch. While Mr.B was shoveling the snow, Tommy was making a perfect snowball. When Mr.B finished his shoveling and was heading back inside, Tommy stood up and threw the snowball as hard as he could toward Mr.B. The snowball went up high and hit a large branch that was covered with snow, which was right on top of Mr.B. The snowball hit the branch and caused a mountain of snow to fall and cover Mr.B and all the sidewalk that was just shoveled. Mr.B looked like a snowman now just standing there covered from head to toe with snow. Seeing this, Tommy started to laugh so hard that he fell to the floor and rolled around holding Teddy. Mr.B yelled at Tommy at the top of his voice, which alerted his Dad and Tommy got in trouble again.

Chapter 3

The following year, after the first snow, Tommy went outside and began to build a snowman with Teddy. Teddy was sitting on a pile of snowballs watching Tommy put the snowman together. As Tommy struggled to lift the head of the snowman on top, Mr.B came out of his front door and said, "You better not try any funny business this year, young man. I see the pile of snowballs over there, you better not throw them." Tommy knew that he had been caught, so he pretended that he was using the snowballs for something else and started to throw them at the snowman. When he was finished building and throwing snowballs at his snowman, Tommy took Teddy and went inside. Tommy spent the rest of the week trying to think of a great prank. Tommy watched Mr.B closely to see what he did and when he went outside. After seeing that Mr.B went outside every morning to get his paper, Tommy came up with a plan. The next day after breakfast, Tommy went outside to play with teddy in the front yard. Tommy and Teddy began to build a fort next to his snowman. They worked hard and long, untill it was finished. The fort had walls that curved into a "C" shape and had walls going almost 3 feet high, which were the perfect size to duck down and hid behind if he ever got in a massive snowball fight.

When the fort was complete, Teddy and Tommy both sat down in the middle of the fort and discussed their plans to prank Mr.B. It was pretty hard to come up with ideas of what to do to prank Mr.B but after a while, Tommy came up with an idea that they were very excited about. It was lunchtime when Mom opened the front door and called Tommy and Teddy inside to eat. After they ate their hard salami sandwiches and baby carrots with apple juice, of course, they went upstairs to their room to lay out the plan in detail and start making preparations for the prank, which would have to be done before dinner time. When they were done discussing their plans, Tommy decided to finish his building block project. After a couple of hours, it was time for Tommy and Teddy to go back outside. Getting dressed, Tommy asked Mom if he could have 2 bottles of water to bring with him outside, for him and Teddy. Tommy took the water bottles and Teddy back to the fort where they talked the plan over. Playing for a bit with the snowman, which became an evil scientist that could only be stopped by hitting him with snowballs; Mom called Tommy in to get ready for dinner and family game night. Tommy screamed, "Ok Mom, I'll be right there, let me get Teddy." When Mom closed the door and went back in, Tommy raced into the fort and grabbed the two water bottles, and ran to

Mr. B's house. Sneaking up the steps on the porch took some stealthy skills, but when he got to the door, Tommy opened one of the bottles and started to pour the water on the floor. He used both bottles to pour water from the front door, down the steps, and on the sidewalk. Then taking the water bottles with him, Tommy ran as fast as he could back into the fort, grabbed Teddy, and headed inside his house. During dinner, Tommy had a big smile on his face and during Family Game night, Tommy tried hard to focus but all he could think about was the Prank. Going to bed, Tommy had a hard time sleeping because all he could think about is waking up in the morning. Tommy knew that he would have to wake up before Mr.B got his morning paper to see the prank in action.

Chapter 4

When the first rays of light hit Tommy's window, he was up. Tommy got up and went to the bathroom to brush his teeth and went back to his room to get dressed. Tommy took Teddy downstairs and ate breakfast as fast as he could. He was so excited about going outside because it had snowed during the night and there was a fresh layer of snow to play in, which made Tommy even more anxious to see if his prank would work. As soon as breakfast was finished, Tommy and Teddy raced outside and slid into the fort, waiting to hear Mr.B opening his door to get the paper. It seemed like forever sitting there waiting, but they finally heard the sound that they were waiting for. Suddenly the door opened and Mr.B stepped outside to get his morning paper. Mr.B was still wearing his pajamas but had a robe over them, which was tied tight around him, and wore brown furry slippers. Mr.B stood in front of the door with his coffee cup in his hand that steamed so much that it looked like it was boiling. Taking a sip of coffee Mr.B took a big breath, shivered a bit, looked around for Tommy, and took a step towards the morning paper which was on the sidewalk. The first step was normal, and Tommy which now had his head above the walls of the fort watching began to think that the prank did not work. The second step was fine as well, but the third step turned into a slide and Mr.B noticed that he was now sliding towards the steps faster and faster. Mr.B dropped his coffee cup and started flailing his hands in the air trying to catch his balance. He was heading towards the steps faster and faster causing him to slide off the steps into the air and into a bush that was covered with snow. Mr.B landed in the bush with a loud crash, which caused the snow on the tree branch above him to come down as well. Mr.B was now in a bush covered with snow, which caused Tommy to stand up and start laughing and dancing with Teddy. All Mr.B could do is sit there angry as he watch Tommy and Teddy laughing. He knew that it was Tommy that did this, so he stood up, still covered with snow, which now made him look like Santa Claus. This made Tommy and Teddy turn and run back home and hide in his room. After hearing the doorbell ring, Tommy knew that he was going to be in trouble again. Spending the next two weeks grounded didn't bother Tommy that much because he knew that he and Teddy played the best prank on Mr.B so far.

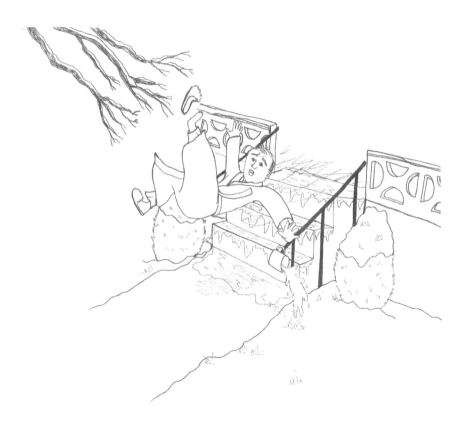

Chapter 5

The next year after the first snow Tommy and Teddy went outside and built a snowman. After finishing the snowman, Teddy took a break and sat on top of the snowman and watched Tommy begin to build their fort. After the fort was finished Tommy and Teddy went inside to think of a plan to prank Mr.B again. Tommy knew that the prank had to be better than the one last year, so he and Teddy sat down to think. Throwing out the ideas which involved robots and big machines, Tommy came up with a great idea. The prank involved a huge snowman, but going outside Tommy realized that there wasn't enough snow to complete the prank that day, so he and Teddy decided to wait for the perfect snow day. They had to wait for a huge snow storm to come before there was enough snow to build the snowman. Taking Teddy, Tommy headed back inside to his room. In his room Tommy sat Teddy down on the bed and began to tell him the plan, "We have to wait for a huge snowfall because we will build a giant snowman right in front of Mr.B's front door. We will make the snowman scary and big to block the front door and scare Mr.B. This will trap Mr.B inside his house and he won't be able to get out his front door." Expaining the plan, Tommy said, "now that we have this great plan, let's go play some video games downstairs," and they went off to play.

After a week of no snow, Tommy was getting worried that his plan to build a snowman in front of Mr.B's door would never happen. As Tommy was staring out the window, from his room, at the front yard which was almost clear from any snow beside the half-melted snowman and fort, he noticed a small white snowflake slowly falling. It looked like a small white feather falling slowly and so gently. Tommy spotted another snowflake, and then another. "It's Snowing, "screamed Tommy. Tommy grabbed Teddy and they both stared out the window as the snowflakes began to multiply. Tommy grabbed Teddy and swung him around in excitement, celebrating the snowfall.

For the rest of the day Tommy, kept going back and forth to the window in his room, watching the snow get bigger and bigger on the ground. That night while in bed, Tommy could not stop thinking of what he had to do. Tommy planned the whole morning out in his head. The plan was simple: build the snowman in smaller pieces and put those pieces together to make one big piece, then continue to do that until the snowman was complete. He would have to carry each piece silently on the porch or Mr.B's house and place them in front of the door. Tommy knew that he had to build the snowman and have it in place before Mr.B would come out to get his paper in the morning, so Tommy had to be up extra early to eat breakfast and go outside. He planned on what he was going to wear and what time he would have to get up, so Tommy set his Robot alarm clock that was on his nightstand by his bed and went to sleep with a smile on his face.

The Alarm clock went off with a robotic voice that said, "Wake Up, Wake Up, Wake up." Tommy jumped out of bed and got dressed and went to the bathroom, and rushed downstairs for breakfast. Tommy and Teddy sat down at the kitchen table and surprised Mom. She knew that Tommy was excited to go out and play in the fresh snow, but because it was earlier than usual, she didn't have breakfast ready for Tommy. Tommy asked for cereal instead of the usual eggs and bacon breakfast because he was in a hurry. Mom prepared his cereal and gave it to him, knowing Tommy's excitement and rush. Tommy ate his cereal so fast that Mom said, "Wow, someone is excited to go play in the fresh snow this morning?" Tommy didn't answer because his mouth was full of cereal so he just nodded. As soon as Tommy finished his cereal he got up and went to get his jacket and boots. Tommy was sitting on the ground putting his boots on, when Mom peaked out of the kitchen and said, "Now you be careful outside, it's slippery. And leave Mr.B alone, don't bother him, Ok?" Tommy answered with, "Uh Hu," as he grabbed Teddy and darted out of the front door.

Tommy turned and ran to the side of the house where his blue sled was leaning up against the house, covered in snow. Shaking the sled off, Tommy placed Teddy on the sled and ran towards the front yard. Tommy started to roll the first snowball, it was perfect packing snow, which made it easy. As soon as the snowball was big enough to pick up with both hands, Tommy picked it up and put it on his sled, and began making another one. When the sled was full of big snowballs Tommy, put Teddy on top and started to pull the sled towards Mr.B's house. Getting to the steps, Tommy knew that he had to be quiet. He picked up the first big snowball and walked up the steps as quietly as he could and placed the first snowball down in front of the front door. Tommy put Teddy next to the front door to keep watch. Tommy continued this process until he had the first part of the snowman complete. Now it was time to make the second ball of the snowman. Tommy decided that the second ball had to be bigger, so he could save time. He rolled the ball on the ground until it was as high as his knees. Then he rolled it onto the sled and pulled it to the steps. It was a little challenging to roll the snowball up the 3 steps onto the porch, but he finally rolled it to the front door and the base of the snowman. Tommy took a deep breath and bent down to pick up the snowball, with all his strength Tommy picked up the snowball and gently placed it on top of the base of the snowman when he heard the front door open.

Chapter 6

Tommy peaked around the snowman and saw Mr.B standing behind the screen door. This startled Tommy; Mr.B yelled, "Hey, what are you doing?" Mr.B tried to open the screen door but it could only open a little bit because of the snowman. Mr.B could only get his hand to come out of the screen door and reach for the snowman. Tommy turned to run away when he realized that Teddy was sitting right next to the door on the floor. Tommy stopped and turned back and looked at Mr.B and then looked at Teddy. Mr.B noticed that Tommy looked at Teddy and he knelt and reached to grab Teddy. Tommy jumped to grab Teddy, but Mr.B grabbed Teddy at the same time. Tommy and Mr.B now both had Teddy in their hands. Tommy had Teddy with both hands by both legs and Mr.B had Teddy by the head with his only hand that was out of the screen door. "Get over here, you little trouble-maker," yelled Mr.B. As the tug-of-war started, Tommy pulled with all his strength and Mr.B held on to Teddy with all his strength as well. Tommy placed his feet on the base of the snowman and pulled as hard as he could to save Teddy's life from the clutches of Mr.B.

With a loud 'RIP" Tommy fell to the ground, Tommy won and got teddy back. Getting to his feet Tommy turned to look at Mr.B who screamed, "Get back here." Tommy turned and began to run home, he leaped off the porch over the steps and landed on the sidewalk, slipped, and landed on the ground. In shock that he fell, Tommy got up to start running again but pain shot up his leg and he fell back to the ground. Tommy screamed in pain and started to cry holding his leg. The front door burst open as Dad came running outside towards Tommy, still in his green and red Pajamas. When Dad got to Tommy, Dad looked at his leg and noticed that it was bent in the wrong position, He knew right away that Tommy had hurt his leg badly. Dad knelt next to Tommy and picked him up. Tommy was crying so hard that it frightened Mr.B and had him frozen in front of the screen door. Dad took Tommy to the car as Mom locked up the house and then got in the car and drove to the Hospital. Seeing what just happened, left Mr.B in shock as he closed the door slowly and went back inside.

Chapter 7

At the Hospital the doctor took Tommy directly to the X-ray room to look at his leg. After a while, the doctor came in with the x-ray in hand and told Tommy and his parents that it was definitely broken. The doctor told Tommy that it would be ok and his leg would heal in about 4 or 5 weeks, but it would have to be put in a cast till then. The Doctor explained to Tommy that a cast was like a hard shell that they would put around his leg to keep it in one place till the bone healed itself. Tommy was scared, but his Mom and Dad told him that they would be next to him the whole time. Tommy took a deep breath and told the Doctor that he was ready for the cast to go on his leg. The Doctor nodded and called two nurses into the room. The nurses brought a bunch of different stuff that were on trays; like cotton wrapping, this stuff that looked like netting, a tub of white gooey stuff, and water. The nurses started by wrapping Tommy's leg with all this stuff that looked very weird to him but made Tommy very curious. Tommy was excited to hear that he was able to choose the color of the cast that would go on his leg. Tommy thought for a while and picked the color Red because that was his favorite color. When the cast was finished getting assembled, the doctor told Tommy and his parents that they would have to stay the night, to make sure that everything was good with the cast and that Tommy would have to learn how to walk on crutches. Tommy was confused about the crutches and wanted to ask the doctor what that meant, but he fell asleep. The next morning Tommy woke up in a hospital room of his own that had a bed and his own TV. His parents were in the room with him sleeping on the couch when the nurse came in with a tray of food for Tommy. After breakfast, Tommy was taken to a special room, where he was given a pair of crutches. He had never seen anything like that, and he was curious what they would do. Maybe they would bounce him up and down or even fly him around, Tommy imagined. The nurse came over to Tommy and gave him a pair of crutches. The nurse demonstrated to Tommy how he was going to use them to walk from now till his leg healed. As Tommy placed the crutches under his armpit, he stood up with his broken leg off the ground. Using the crutches, Tommy began to walk on one leg around the room.

First very slowly, but then after some practice, Tommy became pretty good at walking. Tommy imagined that he now had robot legs, which made him feel cool. As Tommy practiced walking, he pretended that he was a half-robot spy on a secret mission to save the world. This made the practice go by faster and easier for Tommy.

Chapter 8

After Tommy learned to use his new robot legs, his parents were allowed to take him home. Tommy was excited to finally be home again, because he couldn't wait to use his new robot legs to prank Mr.B. When Tommy got back home, he learned that he wasn't allowed to go play outside because the snow would get his cast wet and that was not allowed. Mom was extra worried and acted very protective of Tommy. She kept asking questions like: "Are you feeling good? Do you need anything? Does it hurt?" She kept telling Tommy to stop walking around and to sit down and rest. Tommy spent the day in his room, looking out the window at his snowman, his fort, and at the aftermath of the failed prank in front of Mr.B's house, which hadn't been cleaned up.

Now Mr.B was a sweet old man, and was quite shanken up about what had happened to Tommy. Mr.B couldn't help but feel guilty about Tommy's accident. He tried to tell himself that it wasn't his fault and that it was just an accident, but he still felt bad about Tommy. When Tommy returned from the hospital, Mr.B called right away to find out what happened to Tommy. He apologized to Tommy's parents, but they reassured him that it wasn't his fault, and that it was just an accident. Even though Tommy's parents told him that it wasn't his fault, Mr.B still felt guilty. Mr.B kept replaying that morning's events in his head, which added to his sadness. Mr.B decided to take his mind off of Tommy's accident and decided to go outside and shovel the snow off of his sidewalk since it snowed a little the night before. Mr.B went out the back door since he couldn't open the front screen door due to the unfinished snowman that was there. Mr.B decided to start at the street and shovel towards the house. As he shoveled his way to the stairs, he paused at the spot where Tommy slipped and fell. Pausing for a moment, he took a deep breath and a long sigh and started to shovel the snow on the steps. Then he got up to the patio and started to shovel the unfinished snowman off of the patio, picking up big chunks of snow and throwing them off the patio he noticed something on the ground that caught his eye. Mr.B bent over to pick it up, it was a frozen solid Teddy bear. He quickly realized that it was Tommy's best friend Teddy, but something was missing. Teddy's leg was missing.

He remembered the tug-of-war that he had with Tommy, "It must have broken then", said Mr.B to himself. Turning to the left and right, Mr.B searched for Teddy's leg. He searched the patio, the bushes, the steps, and even his front yard, but nothing. Mr.B couldn't find the leg anywhere. So Mr.B put Teddy in his pocket and finished cleaning up the snowman off the door.

Chapter 9

Getting back inside the house, Mr.B hung his coat and hat and went into the kitchen to pour himself a fresh cup of hot coffee. With Teddy in hand, Mr.B sat down at the kitchen table and stared at Teddy wondering what to do with him. As he was thinking, Mr.B got an idea. A smile grew on his face, he took a long sip of coffee and got up from the table, and headed towards his coat. He put his coat and hat back on and grabbed his wallet from the side table next to his coat rack. Mr.B walked out the front door, locking it behind him, down the steps, towards the street, and headed towards Tommy's house. Mr.B walked past Tommy's house and down the street towards Main Street. It was only a couple of blocks away from the house, but Main Street was located in the center of the little town and had all the stores and shops that people would need. Getting to Main Street Mr.B headed towards a little place called Daniel's Toy Shop. Entering the shop, Mr.B was greeted with a sound of a bell and a warm, "Welcome In", from the shop owner Mr. Daniel. Mr.B said, "Morning", and started his search.

He went down every aisle looking up and down the shelves of toys. Mr.B was looking for a teddy bear that looked like Teddy, but he couldn't find anything. There were dinosaurs, action figures, cars, dolls, games, and all kinds of toys that a kid like Tommy would love, but no teddy bears that looked like Teddy. Disappointed and sad, Mr.B headed towards the door, when something behind the register next to the front door caught his eye. Mr.B asked, "Excuse me, can I see that teddy bear on the back shelf?" Mr. Daniel turned, grabbed the bear, and handed it to Mr.B. The teddy bear was exactly the same size, had the same fur, and looked the same as Teddy, but the color was different. With a great big smile, Mr.B said, "This is perfect, I'll take it." Mr. Daniel was happy to hear and stepped to the register and made the sale for the bear. Putting the teddy bear in a bag and handing it over, Mr. Daniel said, "Great choice, thank you for your business. Have a great day and Merry Christmas." Mr.B replied with a big smile and a warm, "Merry Christmas to you too." Mr.B walked a bit faster on his way home, filled with excitement there was a little more 'pep' in his step as he was holding the bag in his hand. When Mr.B got home, he didn't bother to hang up his coat and hat on the coat rack, he just laid them on the kitchen table along with the bag from the toy store. He began to search the kitchen drawers one by then. Than he moved into the living room, opening every cabinet and drawer he could find. After that, he checked the front closet and then went into his bedroom and searched there. Returning to the kitchen with an old tin cookie container, he sat down on the kitchen chair. Setting the tin container on the table, he removed the new bear from the bag and also took Teddy out of his jacket pocket. He took his jacket and folded it over the chair next to him and turned back to the table and began to work.

Chapter 10

Now Tommy was in his room trying to play with his toys. It was all new now, because of his leg. He couldn't move around like he used to, so everything was a struggle for him. Tommy never seemed to be comfortable, so he started to get agitated. He tired playing with his building blocks but became bored just sitting in one place for a long time. Tommy tired, reading his books, coloring, and even tried playing video games, but all he could think about was going outside. As he looked out the window, the snow began to fall again which made it even harder for him to be in the house. He tried to go back to playing games, but he kept finding himself looking at the window. The falling snow looked so inviting that Tommy couldn't resist but lean against the window and stare outside. Tommy began to dream of playing in the snow and all the fun he would have. He dreamed about his fort and especially about pranking Mr.B. He could imagine laughing at Mr.B covered with snow and how fun that would be. As Tommy was looking out the window daydreaming, Mom opened the door. Seeing Tommy at the window made mom feel a little sad for him, so she tried to lighten up the mood by asking, "Do you want to help me make some chocolate chip brownie cookies, I know they are your favorite?" Tommy turned to his mom and said, "No, I'm not hungry Mom. I just want to be by myself right now." Sadly Mom said, "Ok, but I'll make them anyways so you could have them after dinner for dessert." Tommy nodded and turned back to the window, staring at the falling snow.

Chapter 11

As the days started to drag on, Tommy was getting bored of his toys and games. As he was cleaning up his board games, he realized that Teddy was not in his room. Tommy was so busy figuring out how to get around with his crutches and getting used to his new situation that he forgot about Teddy. Tommy began to search his room: he turned over every toy, emptied his closet, and even crawled under his bed; but no Teddy. Teddy was lost. Tommy was distraught as he slowly made his way downstairs to the living room, where Dad was sitting on the couch reading a book. Tommy cried, "I can't find Teddy anywhere." As Tommy tried to hold back tears, Dad jumped in to help search for Teddy. Dad began his search inside the house looking everywhere that Teddy could have been. Dad then took the search to the garage and looked in the car, but no sign of Teddy. Dad also looked outside in the back yard, the front yard, and even in the leftovers of the fort, but no Teddy. Dad even called the hospital and had the nurses look for Teddy but after looking all over the hospital, there was no sign of Teddy. Tommy couldn't believe that Teddy was gone. He was so sad that he wasn't hungry that night for dinner. Tommy didn't even eat his favorite chocolate chip brownie cookies either. He was too sad to eat.

After dinner, Tommy slowly slunk up the stairs to get ready for bed. Seeing Tommy so sad, Mom had an idea. "Would you like to go down to the toy store tomorrow to try to find another toy?" Mom asked carefully. She knew that nothing could replace Teddy, but didn't like seeing Tommy so sad. Immediately Tommy said, "NO, I just want Teddy", as he slid into bed slowly. Seeing Tommy so sad, Mom came and gave him a big hug. She kissed him good night and tucked him in. "Well, if you change your mind, let me know in the morning", said Mom as she closed the door. Tommy couldn't sleep all night because he kept thinking about Teddy, wondering where he could be and how sad he was being lost. That night Tommy dreamt about himself and Teddy building snowmen and a fort.

Chapter 12

In the morning, Tommy woke up still sad and missing Teddy. During breakfast, Mom asked Tommy if he wanted to go to the toy store again, but Tommy said "no." Mom explained to Tommy that he wasn't going to the toy store to replace Teddy, but to just get another toy because he was bored with his old ones. After some hesitation, Tommy agreed to go with his Mom to the toy store. Tommy finished his breakfast and got dressed to go. As the front door opened and the cold air hit Tommy, a smile began to grow on his face. Even though it took a while to get to the car, Tommy was enjoying the outside air and just being able to leave the house. Getting in the car, Mom and Tommy headed towards Main Street to Daniels Toy Shop. As Tommy entered the toy shop, his eyes began to open wide with the possibilities of all the new toys. Tommy slowly staggered down each aisle and took his time to look at every toy on the shelves. "You can get anything you want, just don't go crazy," said mom in a loud voice from across the shop.

Mom was talking to the toy shop owner across the counter. Tommy was even more excited because he knew that he could get a new toy. As Tommy went down the aisles, he tried to decide what he wanted. He looked at all the toys that he liked, but there were so many options to choose from: action figures, cars, board games, video games, swords, toy guns, and even building block sets. The only thing that Tommy could think about was Teddy. He missed Teddy more and more as he looked around. He knew in his heart that nothing could replace Teddy. Even after checking the stuffed animal section, there wasn't another stuffed animal that could replace Teddy. He finally decided to get a video game, thinking he could get his mind off of losing Teddy.

After paying for the game, Tommy and Mom went back to the car and headed home. Making a quick stop to get Mom some coffee, they finally arrived home. Slowly getting back inside the house, Tommy took his coat off and went in to play his new game. The game was a temporary distraction from losing Teddy, but it helped a bit.

Chapter 13

After a couple of days, right before dinner, Tommy was sitting on the couch in front of the TV trying to beat the last level of the video game that he just got. The doorbell rang, but Tommy paid no attention to it and kept playing. Mom and Dad were setting up the dinner table when they heard the doorbell ring again. Dad stopped placing the plates on the table and headed for the door saying, "I wonder who that could be?" Tommy paused the game when he saw Dad going to the door. He wondered who it could be because Dad called Mom over to the door as well and they both were talking to someone. After a short while, Mom turned to Tommy and said, "We have a guest for dinner tonight Tommy." As Mom and Dad stepped back from the door, Tommy was surprised to see Mr.B enter the house. Confusion washed over Tommy's face, as he didn't know what to do and say. Suddenly all these questions flooded his brain: Why is Mr.B here? What did he want? Am I going to get in trouble for something? Mr.B came in and handed Mom a bouquet of flowers, which made Mom smile. Tommy then noticed that Mr.B was holding a box in his other hand, which was wrapped in some weird-looking brown paper. Mom gave Tommy a stern gaze, which Tommy knew what it meant automatically. Tommy got up on his crutches and went to greet Mr.B.

Chapter 14

Sitting at the dinner table together was very awkward for Tommy. Dad, Mom, and Mr.B seemed to be having a great time. They were laughing together and telling stories. Tommy sat in silence just staring at what was happening, like watching a movie. Tommy was waiting to hear Mr.B say something that would get him in trouble, but nothing was happening. Tommy just sat there very suspicious of Mr.B, so he just ate his food in silence. Mr.B turned to Tommy and asked him about his leg, but Mom answered all the questions. Tommy just sat there eating his food, staring at them. Once everyone was finished eating, Mr.B thanked Mom for the 'wonderful dinner.' Then he turned to Tommy and said, "I came here tonight to give you a present. I wanted to help you feel better." Mr.B bent over and took the brown wrapped box from under his chair and handed it to Tommy. Tommy took the box and stared at his parents. "Go ahead and open it," said Mom. Tommy looked at Mr.B, which had a smile on his face, and then back at the box. With a slight shrug, Tommy started to open the box. As he tore the brown wrapping paper, Tommy discovered a plain brown cardboard box underneath. "What could it be," Tommy thought to himself as he peeled back the tape that was holding the box shut. Tommy opened the flaps of the box and reached in grabbed what was inside and pulled it out. "TEDDY," screamed Tommy immediately hugging his friend.

"You found Teddy," Tommy said as the box fell to the floor. Tommy finished hugging Teddy and holding him up when he suddenly froze. Something was different about Teddy.

As Tommy was holding Teddy up, Mom let out a gasp and began to cry. As Tommy was looking at Teddy, the memory of what happened that day when he broke his leg became clear in his mind. Tommy replayed the memory and remembered that Teddy had his leg ripped off when he was having the Tug-of-war with Mr.B during the prank in front of Mr.B's door with the snowman. Snapping back to reality at the dinner table, Tommy noticed that Teddy's leg wasn't missing. Teddy's leg was back on, but it was red. Just like his cast. Tears began to swell up in Tommy's eyes as he realized that Teddy was just like him. Tommy looked at Mr.B and took his crutches and walked over to him. When he got around the table to Mr.B, Tommy dropped his crutches and fell into his arms and hugged him. As Mr.B and Tommy hugged they both started to cry.

This made Mom and Dad cry as well. The tears lasted but a moment, a sweet and tender moment. Tommy sat down right next to Mr.B for the rest of the night. The night lasted for what seemed like forever. Everyone talked together, laughed, and joked. Mom served cookies and milk for everyone and Mr.B even retold the stories of all the pranks that Tommy played on him. With laughter and joy, Tommy and Mr.B became friends. As the night ended, Mr.B and Tommy said their goodbyes and hugged again. That night in bed, Tommy and Teddy dreamed, planning and prepping for the start of the next winter war.

The End

Cristian Lascau

Cristian Lascau resides in Phoenix with his wife Renee and his two children Hope and Oliver. Born in Romania but grew up in the United States, Cristian has always had a passion for stories. He is an actor, writer, and works in construction. Cristian loves spending his free time with his family and dog Theo, adventuring the outdoors, and especially loves fishing.

Emma Rusnac

Emma Rusnac lives in Phoenix, AZ with her husband and three children. Originally from the UK, Emma has always had a passion for art, starting in her early childhood. She studied Art & Design in collage and later went to do a illustration school in Kona, Hawaii. Her primary medium is acrylics but has experience working with many different mediums. She loves the challange of bringing a story visually to life. When she's not creating, she loves spending time with family, being outdoors in nature and eating yummy food!

Thank You

Lightning Source UK Ltd.
Milton Keynes UK
UKHW020037070223
416580UK00005B/505